The Christmas Poop Plan

Emily Smith and
Martin Smith

Illustrated by

Philip Knibbs

ISBN: 9781077453753

For Bertie and Jude

Contents

Acknowledgments

1. Elves   1

2. Pupstar   5

3. Aunt Maude   11

4. Middle of the night   16

5. Soggy slippers   22

6. Squishy cereal   26

7. The Poop Plan   30

8. Guzzle guts   36

9. Christmas Eve   40

10. Angel eyes   46

11. Nick of time   51

12. Oh no!   55

13. Gotcha   63

14. Christmas Morning 69

About the authors

About the illustrator

Acknowledgments

Emily has always wanted to write a book with her dad.

This is that book.

With Martin busy working on the Charlie Fry series, it was Emily who came up with the characters and the plot for the Poop Plan. Not bad for a seven-year-old, who prefers maths to writing.

Of course, it helps when a story is supported with wonderful illustrations.

And there's no doubt the Poop Plan has been brought to life brilliantly by Phil Knibbs.

Several other people have contributed to helping create the Christmas Poop Plan too.

Richard Wayte did his usual proofreading masterclass, providing an extra pair of eyes on the wording.

Comedy genius Alicia Babaee somehow managed to take time out of her busy globe-trotting schedule to edit the words too.

We also had helping hands from River Amey, Henry Herlihy, Jessica and Emmeline Kilpin, who read an early version of the book and provided great feedback.

And finally, thank you to you for reading.

Always, always believe.

1. ELVES

Elves are naughty.
Some can be kind.
But most are pests.
Scamps. Tinkers. Sneaks.
I know it.
You know it.
Everyone knows it.
Wherever there's trouble in the world, most of the time I bet you will find an elf at the bottom of it.
Have you ever had new felt tip

pens mysteriously run out overnight?

Bingo. Elves love colouring. And they never put the lids back on either.

Have you woken up to find a string of crusty bogies wiped on your pillow?

Yep, elves again.

And always, always check your chocolate-coated breakfast cereal carefully.

Why? Elves love to poop and hide it.

But the three elves living at 181 Ashby Close are different.

They are mean.

They are horrid.

And they are disgusting too.

What's that?

You don't believe me?

You didn't really think all elves were wonderful and magical, did you?

Wrong!

And Stanky, Cranky and Planky are some of the very worst.

In fact, I bet this bunch are the naughtiest creatures on the planet.

They hatched a plan so evil that it would make your mouth fall wide open for a day.

Perhaps even longer.

But, before we begin, I want you to remember this: for every naughty thing that happens, there is twice as much good in the world.

And a special Christmas miracle was needed to stop this bunch of stinkers in their tracks.

This is that tale.

2. PUPSTAR

Our story begins a week before Christmas Eve.

Little Johnny Gibbs and his sister Catherine heard a car door slam and raced to peer out of the window.

Dad was home from work.

The children waved as they watched their father get out of his car holding a large box with a blanket over it.

"What's he carrying?" Johnny

asked.

Stan Gibbs walked past the twinkling Christmas lights in the bushes outside 181 Ashby Close, heading towards the front door with a big smile on his face.

The door was open in a flash.

Johnny had short, wild hair that made it look like he'd been running.

And, in fact, Johnny DID run everywhere.

So, it was no surprise when he reached the front door first.

The boy's eyes were open wide with excitement: "Hi Dad!

"What have you got there? Is it something for us? What is it?"

Tall with brown hair, Stan laughed at the string of questions being asked.

"Hello children.

"Quiet please, and let's say a big hello to the newest member of our family."

Stan pulled off the blanket to reveal a cage.

Behind the bars was a trembling puppy.

"Johnny and Catherine. Meet Archie. He is only eight weeks old, very young and shy.

"And he needs lots of love and attention.

"This is my Christmas present to the family."

Archie had brown fur and a waggy tail.

He looked scared.

Johnny and Catherine squealed.

They had always wanted a dog.

Archie was perfect.

Dad gently opened the cage and urged the kids to give the puppy a little space.

Slowly Archie crept forward and sniffed Catherine's hand.

Catherine was two years older than Johnny.

She had long hair that tickled Archie's nose as she bent over him.

His tongue felt warm and tickly as he nibbled her fingers.

Slowly Catherine picked Archie up and gave him a hug.

That did the trick.

Feeling a little more confident, Archie came to life and gave her face a giant lick.

As Catherine rolled on the floor giggling, the little puppy turned towards Johnny and jumped on

him too.
Everyone laughed.

Archie was perfect.

The whole family loved him.
Apart from one person.
A horrible shriek came from the hallway.
"What on earth is that?"

3. AUNT MAUDE

Aunt Maude had come to live with the Gibbs family last year.

Dad had a new job making giant underpants and had to travel a long distance every day.

So, he asked his sister to look after the children before and after school, which Aunt Maude did with A LOT of grumbling.

She was the meanest person the kids had ever met.

The old woman cackled like a

witch and had extremely long fingers that were always cold – even in summer.

Her hair was a horrible purple colour and she stank of talcum powder.

And she hated animals.

Cute kittens? She wanted to chase them away with a broom.

Pretty goldfish?

Her eyes sparkled as she talked about the best ways to cook them.

Hamsters?

They were nothing more than giant rats, according to Aunt Maude.

And dogs were her biggest enemy.

Especially puppies.

"Dogs? They smell. They scratch.

They bite.

"They ruin everything … and there is nothing worse than a stinky puppy," shrieked Aunt Maude from the doorway.

Archie did not understand, of course.

The puppy ran towards the woman making strange sounds, wanting to be friends.

Aunt Maude screamed loud enough to wake up the entire street.

"AWFUL MONSTER!

"Shoo. Shoo!

"Get away from me, you beastly thing. Stanley, you know I don't like dogs."

Archie froze in shock and then ran away from the crazy lady at full speed.

He hid behind the small coffee table, trembling.

Dad spoke quickly: "I know you don't like dogs too much, Maude, but the kids have wanted a puppy for a long time.

"After the year they've had, they deserve an early Christmas treat.

"Please try to get along with Archie.

"He is one of the family now."

Johnny scooped up Archie and snuggled the puppy, who was looking tired.

Aunt Maude snorted.

"I'll give the little beast one chance.

"If he does one thing wrong, then he will have to go!"

4. MIDDLE OF THE NIGHT

After a great deal of fussing over the puppy, the Gibbs house went to bed.

Archie was fast asleep before Johnny and Catherine had even brushed their teeth.

Soon everyone was tucked up in bed.

Nothing stirred.

Except for the small figure

walking carefully along the top of the lounge radiator.

Cranky the elf carried a full tube of toothpaste in his tiny hands.

He was one of three elves that lived in the Gibbs house, along with Planky and Stanky.

They arrived years ago when Johnny was a baby.

And they had been causing mischief ever since.

Some elves got caught when they were up to no good.

But this lot were too clever.

They had never been caught.

And that had made them naughtier than ever.

Eyes gazing upwards, Stanky stood at the bottom of the radiator.

She whispered to her brother:

"Quick. Pass it down here."

The plan was simple: they would fill Aunt Maude's slipper with toothpaste.

Then – and this is the really sneaky part – they would place the empty tube inside Johnny's room so the boy would get the blame.

Johnny – despite being asleep – would be in big trouble.

And the elves would laugh quietly as Meanie Maude (as they called her) exploded with anger.

They loved winding up the miserable goat. It was one of many jokes they'd played on her.

These elves were crafty.

In the daytime, they pretended to be normal toys, happy to be flung around by the kids.

Then, at night when the house was asleep, the games would begin.

If someone did come downstairs during the night, the elves simply flopped down and waited to be found.

The humans were stupid.

With no-one telling them off, Cranky, Stanky and Planky were getting worse and worse.

They were more evil than ever.

They loved upsetting Aunt Maude because she turned a funny colour of red when she was angry.

This made her their favourite target.

Cranky dropped the tube of toothpaste down to Stanky, who hung it over the edge of the slipper.

Then Planky climbed up onto the tube and began jumping up and down to force the gooey white paste out.

They sang quietly as they worked:

"We are the elves of Ashby Close.
"And we love to be super gross.
"Aunt Maude is an nasty old goat.
"When she screams, we sit and gloat!"

The trio cackled as the toothpaste oozed into the slipper.

When the tube was empty, they would put the slipper in Aunt Maude's room and place the empty toothpaste tube under Johnny's pillow – and wait for the fun to begin tomorrow.

But then something happened the elves did not expect.

Archie barked.

5. SOGGY SLIPPERS

"My beautiful slipper!

"What has that little beast done?

"That dog has got to go!"

Aunt Maude's hair was in curlers and her bright pink nightie was crumpled.

She looked like a giant pink dessert with sprinkles on top.

Dad put a finger to his lips.

"Ssshhh. You'll wake the kids if you scream like that."

Aunt Maude stopped talking but

still looked wild.

Archie ignored the crazy lady.

He was busy sniffing around the slipper and empty tube of toothpaste.

He growled gently at the elves, who had dropped to the floor as soon as the light went on.

Aunt Maude whispered: "That wretch has ruined my wonderful slipper! He's filled it ... with toothpaste! What a sneak!"

She flung the three elves – dressed in their green and red outfits – aside as she picked up her gooey slipper.

Dad chuckled.

"He's a puppy, Maude. Archie may have stolen your slipper but he couldn't fill it with toothpaste. He is only a dog!"

Maude looked at the puppy with narrow eyes. His nose was still covered in toothpaste after sniffing around.

"How do explain this nonsense then, if it is not the beast?"

Dad shrugged.

"I don't know. But it is too late to worry about that now.

"I need to settle Archie down again – because I have a busy day at work tomorrow and I would like some sleep!"

Aunt Maude huffed once, turned around and stomped back to her bedroom.

Dad opened the kitchen door for the puppy to go into the garden for a wee.

But Archie wasn't interested in going outside.

He was too busy sniffing around Cranky, who had ended up underneath the sofa.

Dad scooped up the toy away from Archie and picked up the other two elves as well.

He placed them high up on a shelf, well out of Archie's reach.

Then he grabbed the puppy, who was quietly growling at the elves, and they headed outside.

"Come on boy. Leave the elves alone. Time to go to the toilet, so we can all get back to bed.

"We need some sleep."

Up on the shelf, the elves looked at each other in shock. Archie had caught them out.

With a terrible grin, Planky whispered: "The mutt has got to go."

6. SQUISHY CEREAL

Everyone was up early.

No-one dared to mention the toothpaste incident.

Aunt Maude glared at Archie – who was hiding behind the coffee table again – but did not say a word.

Johnny and Catherine were going to school. Dad had already left for work.

Before she walked the kids to school, Maude had to finish her breakfast.

She had her own special cereal that no-one else was allowed to touch.

It was a funny brown colour.

And soggy. And rather yucky.

It smelled disgusting.

To Catherine's eyes, the breakfast cereal looked like small pieces of wet cardboard.

Johnny was convinced it was rabbit poop.

Maude licked the spoon clean as she swallowed the last mouthful of the revolting mixture.

"Delicious as ever! The only way to start a morning," she cried in the direction of the children, who had finished their own breakfasts and now were busy playing with Archie.

"Yes, Aunt Maude," they replied together.

Archie was put into his cage and, with a lot of sighing, Aunt Maude agreed to be kind to the puppy while the others were out.

No-one paid any attention to the elves sitting high up on the shelf.

Aunt Maude barked out her orders and within minutes the kids were ready to leave.

Thirty seconds later, Aunt Maude grabbed her expensive leather handbag and they set off.

The house fell quiet.

Cranky twisted round.

He spoke in a low voice so Archie would not hear them: "Pssst! We have to act fast.

"You know what we need to do."

Planky nodded, understanding straight away.

But Stanky was confused.

"Errrmmmm.…"

Cranky took a long look at the sleeping puppy.

He whispered: "We have to get rid of that … thing … down there.

"He could ruin everything – especially when he gets bigger.

"This means we need to act fast.

"We need to go big."

Stanky gasped.

"Really?"

Cranky and Planky nodded together. They had a wicked look in their eyes.

Cranky added: "Oh, yes. It's time for the Poop Plan."

7. THE POOP PLAN

The Poop Plan was simple.

It was also gross.

But these were horrible elves at 181 Ashby Close.

They had been hatching the plot for months – ever since that witch Aunt Maude had arrived in their kingdom.

Now was the time for the Poop Plan.

They would eat.

And eat.

And eat some more.
Until they thought they would
burst.

Then they would poop.

That's right. Elf poop looks like tiny pellets – like rabbit dung.

They would fill Aunt Maude's glasses case with all the poop that they'd stored up.

The old dragon loved her glasses. They hoped the trick might tip the old goose over the edge – and convince her to return to her own house. Or wherever she came from.

But now the elves needed to get Archie into big trouble too.

So, they added an extra twist.

One of them – Planky – was always hungry. He would eat more than the other two.

Much more.

He would keep eating until his green and red coat began to

stretch and he felt like he was going to pop.

After a week of gobbling up everything he could find, Planky would create a giant poop – the biggest dung an elf had ever created.

And then he would dump it into Aunt Maude's precious handbag.

The pile of stink would be so enormous that Archie would be blamed.

Aunt Maude would explode, at the very least.

Christmas would be ruined … and Dad would have no choice but to get rid of the dog.

And, if everything went to plan and Maude left as well, then they would have full control of the house again.

The elves sniggered.

It was perfect.

They would say goodbye to the mangy puppy, and perhaps even Aunt Maude, in a single wonderful day.

Christmas Day.

Now they had to prepare.

It was midnight as they climbed down from the shelf towards the kitchen, looking to find food that would not be missed.

They sang:

"Eat, eat, we'll eat all night long.
"Our Poop Plan can never go wrong!
"Then we'll poop, poop, poop,
"We'll cover the mad lady in goop,
"And get rid of the doggy – whoop, whoop!"

The elves cackled with glee. They thought no-one knew about their plan.

But they were wrong.

Someone watched silently as the wicked trio danced into the kitchen and out of sight.

Once the elves had gone, the eyes looked down towards the puppy, sleeping peacefully.

"I think this house needs a little Christmas miracle," said the watcher.

8. GUZZLE GUTS

Have you ever been into a kitchen cupboard?

I don't mean grabbing the biscuit tin.

Or fishing out a handful of yummy snacks and heading straight back to your toys.

I'm talking about kneeling down and going right to the very back – in the darkest corners that even grown-ups forget about.

Those cupboard corners are

strange places.

They are dark.

They are dusty.

And they are always full of food that no-one wants to eat.

You know the type – the yucky stuff that mums and dads say is good for us but no-one actually likes, even old people.

Tins of pilchards.

An old pot of mustard.

There will definitely be some corned beef.

Or dried mushrooms.

Perhaps a few loose sprouts that had been missed last Christmas.

Yuck.

These things lurk in our houses and we don't even know it.

Once a year, mums and dads may decide to have a clear out – and throw the mouldy food away.

But the Gibbs family had not done this in ages.

With the excitement of Christmas, Dad had forgotten about the disgusting stuff sitting at the back of their cupboards.

But the elves hadn't.

And this horrible grub was perfect for the Poop Plan.

All they had to do was eat it.

So, they began to tuck in.

Every night for the next week, they guzzled as much awful food as they could fit into their tiny tummies.

They gobbled liquorice sweets with fluff on.

Pickled onions left over from last Christmas went down the hatch.

Banana chips that were so

ancient the elves thought their teeth might snap? They were scoffed quickly too.

For six nights, the elves ate themselves silly.

They could barely eat another thing.

Planky felt sick all the time but he kept eating until the end.

Now they were ready.

They were set to ruin Christmas.

9. CHRISTMAS EVE

It was the night before Christmas.

Everything was ready.

Presents had been placed underneath the tree.

The turkey sat in the kitchen fridge, ready to be cooked for lunch.

Stockings had been hung for the arrival of Santa.

Children across the world were super excited, all set for the big day they had waited so long for.

The Christmas tree stood in the corner of the room with a huge fairy sitting on top.

Archie was snoring gently in his cage.

The elves only had a few minutes to put their evil plan into action.

Santa had not reached the Gibbs house yet.

They knew that if Father Christmas discovered their little game, he would stop it.

Santa did not like tricks — especially mean ones.

The elves needed to move quickly.

Unfortunately, Planky was now enormous. He used to be a thin, mean elf with a neat jacket and hat.

Not any more.

He was still mean, of course.

But now he was huge. He had a small head and a round body that looked like a bowling ball.

The buttons had popped off his

jacket as his tummy had swelled to a gigantic size.

His hat was missing too. It had not been able to fit for days.

He was five times the size of the other elves, even though they were much bigger too.

But Planky was … massive.

He was packed with poop.

In fact, he was so big that he could not walk.

How would they get him down to Aunt Maude's handbag, which sat in the doorway between the kitchen and lounge?

Cranky and Stanky looked at each other.

There was one thing to do.

They would roll Planky along the shelf and push him off the edge.

He would not like it — so they

didn't bother to tell him.

Instead Cranky and Stanky simply stepped behind him and together gave him a hard push.

"Arrrgggghhhh!" Planky shouted as he fell to the ground with a thud.

The elves giggled as they climbed down after their brother.

Within seconds, they reached the floor.

Cranky switched on the table lamp and helped Stanky roll Planky – who was complaining about being pushed off the shelf – towards the handbag.

In a flash, Stanky removed the glasses case, which had Aunt Maude's reading glasses inside.

Cranky wiped his brow. Rolling Planky had been hard work.

It was worth it though.

The plan was nearly complete.

He was joined by Stanky at the glasses case while Planky hauled himself onto the edge of Aunt Maude's expensive handbag.

They were ready.

Cranky whispered: "You know what to do. It's Poop Time."

10. ANGEL EYES

As we said earlier, elves are mean.

They are rascals.

Pests.

But the elves at Ashby Close had spent so long making the great Poop Plan that they did not realise they were being watched.

Every night, a pair of eyes had followed the wicked trio's plan to get rid of Archie and Aunt Maude.

The angel sitting on the top of the tree was not going to let these mean idiots ruin Christmas for everyone.

While the elves were busy pooping, the Christmas angel put her own plan into action.

A quick flick of her wand awoke Catherine in her bedroom upstairs.

As Catherine rubbed her eyes, still half asleep, a kind voice spoke to her.

"Come downstairs quickly, my dear. You are needed."

Catherine shook her head.

Was she dreaming?

What was the time?

Had Santa been already?

Perhaps Santa needed her help?

The voice spoke again.

"Hurry, Catherine! Archie needs you!"

Archie?

Catherine was wide awake now.

She jumped out of bed and pulled on her fluffy dressing gown and slippers.

Catherine slowly opened her bedroom door so it did not creak and wake up Dad.

She slid out and paused outside Johnny's room. Should she wake him up too? No, she decided.

Johnny would never get back to sleep again if she woke him now.

It was Christmas Eve and getting her excited little brother to sleep earlier had been hard enough.

Anyway, she wasn't even sure why she was going downstairs herself.

But the strange voice had insisted – so down she went.

Slowly.

One of the stairs creaked.

Catherine knew one made a sound but she always forgot which one.

And in the middle of the night, it sounded so loud.

She paused to see if her dad – or even worse Aunt Maude – had been woken up because of the noise.

Silence. Nothing happened so Catherine continued slowly down the stairs.

At the bottom, she pushed open the door to the lounge.

It was dark inside and, without a second thought, Catherine flicked the light switch on.

And she gasped at the awful scene inside.

11. NICK OF TIME

Something was wrong.

One of the stairs had creaked loudly.

Cranky had heard that sound a million times before.

This was dangerous.

Someone was awake.

Footsteps.

And they were coming downstairs.

Cranky's eyes widened. For the first time ever, they were going to get caught.

He pulled up his trousers and barked at Stanky.

"Grab Planky and get back on the shelf! Hurry!

"Someone is coming!"

Their part of the Poop Plan was complete.

From the horrible grunts and groans coming from Planky's direction, he was nearly done too.

They would have to leave the bag in the doorway.

Cranky leapt up to the lamp and switched it off.

It meant he would have to cross the room in the dark, but he didn't have a choice.

There was no time.

"Hey! We can't see!"

Stanky called out to her brother but Cranky ignored her.

They only had a few seconds.

Cranky jumped off the table and … slipped over straight away.

Urggh! Poop!

Some poop must have spilled out of the bag and now Cranky was covered in it.

Trying to ignore the horrible pong, Cranky staggered to Archie's cage.

Using all his strength, he pulled the lock and pushed open the door.

Archie kept snoring.

That mutt could sleep through an earthquake, the elf thought.

Cranky pulled an evil grin.

The Poop Plan was finally complete.

The footsteps started again.

The sounds were soft but they were getting louder.

Cranky ran as fast as he could.

He jumped up on to the white couch, ignoring the horrible smell.

Then he climbed up onto one of the sofa's arms before quickly jumping onto the shelves.

In a flash he was next to the other elves. Planky was already looking A LOT slimmer.

They had done it.

Now all they had to do was sit on the shelf and wait for the fireworks.

Seconds later, Catherine opened the door and turned the light on.

12. OH NO!

Catherine gasped in horror.

The living room stank.

The pong was awful … it smelt just like poop.

Her eyes widened.

It was poop. Gross!

Catherine's mouth fell open as she saw Aunt Maude's expensive handbag covered in poop.

The leather was smeared in brown stinky stuff.

And the revolting smell made her feel sick.

She turned towards Archie's cage.

It was unlocked and the cage door was wide open.

Somehow their puppy had managed to escape, although he was back in there sleeping now.

"Oh no," she whispered. "What have you done this time, naughty little boy?"

Catherine knew Aunt Maude would go bananas. Worse still, she would want to get rid of Archie.

They had waited so long for a puppy – and now they were going to lose their wonderful pet even before Christmas had arrived!

"It's not fair!" Catherine said to herself. "Puppies are always naughty. They don't mean to be – it is part of growing up.

"All I want for Christmas is to keep Archie!"

Up on the shelf, the elves looked at each other and smiled.

This had not been part of the plan.

But if Catherine woke up the entire house in the middle of the night, then the dog may be leaving even earlier than they had thought.

This was excellent. They kept watching, loving every moment.

Catherine stopped talking as the strange voice spoke again inside her head.

"Wait, my dear. Not everything is as it seems. Look a little closer. Start near to your feet."

Catherine did not know where the voice was coming from.

She was alone.

But she listened and dropped

down to the floor.

Archie was asleep. Surely if he had escaped from his cage, he wouldn't have got back in and fallen asleep?

It did not make sense.

Catherine looked closely at the unlocked door.

And then she saw the clues.

Little footprints made from poop.

They were tiny.

No wonder she had missed them.

Catherine twirled around.

Yes! There!

They started near the handbag and headed to Archie's cage.

The mystery voice spoke again.

"Follow the trail. Those footsteps will reveal who is really behind this ghastly mess."

Using her finger, Catherine traced the marks away from the cage and towards the sofa. With a big yawn, Archie came out of the cage to join her, sniffing the footprints.

The poop trail led across the couch and on to one of the arms. And then it stopped.

Catherine looked around for another sign.

The voice spoke again: "Follow your nose. They are right there."

Catherine nodded.

She started at the bottom shelf and worked her way up – sniffing all the time to try to find the owner of the yucky footsteps.

If anyone came into the room at that very moment, they would think she was quite mad.

She was sniffing bookshelves in the middle of the night – moments before Santa was due to arrive.

Catherine did not care though.

She needed to find out who did this horrible thing to their house.

The problem was the smell of poop was everywhere.

And then she saw them.

The three elves sitting together on the top shelf.

"Surely not," Catherine said. "Elves aren't real, are they?"

The voice answered her: "Check their feet! That will tell you!"

Catherine grabbed the biggest elf first.

He looked … well … a bit shabby. He had no hat and his

clothes were ragged.

But his feet were clean.

The second elf – who was far more smartly dressed – was clean too.

That only left the third.

Holding two elves in one hand, she grabbed Cranky in the other and sniffed his feet.

Ewww! The smell!

It was disgusting.

Then she spotted it.

A spot of poop was still stuck to the rascal's feet.

Catherine could not believe her eyes. It was the elves!

They had made all this mischief.

And then … Cranky kicked her on the nose.

13. GOTCHA

"Ouch!"

Catherine was so shocked that she nearly dropped the elves.

"Let me go!"

Cranky sneered as his legs kicked out wildly.

But Catherine did not let go.

Instead she gripped the gang even tighter.

The elf's foot was small so the kick did not hurt — but it

surprised her.

Catherine's face turned almost purple with anger.

"You … evil … little … monsters. Look at the mess you've caused."

Catherine looked around.

The piles of poop.

The unlocked cage.

The sleeping puppy.

Suddenly she understood.

She whispered: "You wanted us to find this.

"And you … knew we would blame poor Archie.

"Oooh, you horrible little beasts. So this is why he's been barking at you!"

She yelped as Cranky bit her finger.

Planky and Stanky were now

struggling too, all trying to escape.

But Catherine shook her head.

"You horrible lot do not deserve to spend another night in this house. In fact, you need to be taught a lesson."

She walked over to the fireplace and pulled down her own stocking and thrust the elves inside.

They fought, of course.

Stanky, Planky and Cranky did not like being trapped in the dark – unable to cause mischief.

But Catherine's hand was wrapped around the top of the stocking so none of them could escape.

She looked around the living room, which was covered in

ghastly smelling poop.

"How am I going to clean all this up before Santa arrives? He can't see this! And what happens if Auntie Maude finds out?"

The voice in her head spoke for a final time.

"Leave everything to me, my dear. You look after our little elfish devils and get to bed.

"Hurry now. Santa will be here soon. Well done. You have saved Christmas."

Catherine beamed.

"Thank you so much. Whoever you are!"

Still holding the bag of wriggling elves, she skipped into the kitchen.

There was only one place these elves would be spending

Christmas.
Where they could cause as little mischief as possible.

They were still fighting as Catherine opened the washing

machine door.

Without a word, she chucked all three into the washing machine with a thud.

Before they could complain or escape, Catherine slammed the door shut and set the machine for a long rinse.

She smiled to herself as the machine began to fill with water and turn the wailing elves upside down.

Over and over again.

14. CHRISTMAS MORNING

Torn wrapping paper covered the floor. Santa had visited the Gibbs household.

Johnny had been up early and ripped open his presents in a few moments.

Catherine followed, yawning.

She looked around the lounge.

The room was perfect. Something magical had happened.

Aunt Maude's handbag was spotless.
There was no poop anywhere.
Or disgusting smells.
Apart from Archie's usual morning slobber.

The puppy bounced around, highly excited although he had no idea what was going on.

He proudly held a new ball in his jaws – his own gift from Father Christmas.

Even Aunt Maude looked happy. She was busy squealing with joy after opening a furry yellow and brown scarf.

Santa had been.

Everyone was excited.

And the Poop Plan had failed.

The washing machine was still going, Catherine realised.

She walked out to the kitchen and smiled.

Then she pressed the repeat button on the machine again.

Those awful elves could spend

another couple of hours getting clean before they were moved.

Catherine had already found a giant biscuit tin and – with the help of some sticky tape – she intended to give the elves a new home.

"Merry Christmas, sweetheart. Why is the washing machine on? I thought I heard it last night."

Dad appeared in the kitchen, scratching his head.

Catherine shrugged.

"I think Archie may have had a little accident, Dad. Don't worry, I cleared it up before anyone else discovered it."

Dad gave her a big hug as they walked back into the living room. He whispered in her ear: "Well done. You know how some things can be ... difficult ... to explain to some people."

Catherine wanted to tell him everything – but did not. Instead, she nodded.

"Yes, Dad. No problem."

And as she turned to talk to Johnny, the fairy on top of the Christmas tree gave her a small smile and a cheeky wink.

Catherine's mouth fell open with surprise but, in the blink of an eye, the fairy was still again.

Catherine smiled to herself.

Christmas had been saved.

They had done it.

SIX MONTHS LATER

Elves don't like water.

In fact, they hate being wet.

By now Stanky, Cranky and Planky were the cleanest elves in the country after being stuck in the washing machine for two whole days.

Sometimes they still feel dizzy from all the sploshing and splashing.

But their punishment did not end there.

Oh no.

They had been far too naughty for that.

After their 29th rinse in the washing machine, Catherine moved them to their new home – the garden shed.

It was boiling hot during the day and freezing at night.

And dark.

Full of spiders.

It smelt funny too.

The elves were arguing – as usual.

That awful girl had wrapped sticky tape around the three of them to keep them together.

Then Catherine had plonked them inside the old biscuit tin –

and wrapped the lid tightly so there could be no escape.

The elves struggled to get free but nothing had worked so far.

So, they laid there every day, unable to escape and arguing all the time.

"This is your fault, Cranky."

"No, it isn't! Planky is to blame!"

"I haven't done anything. The Poop Plan was a terrible idea."

"I hate this tin!"

The arguments never stopped.

Sometimes the tin shook as the elves tried to fight each other – but the sticky tape meant they could not move their arms or legs.

The Christmas Poop Plan had failed.

They had been forgotten by

everyone.

Except for Archie.

The puppy, who was now much bigger, was forever sniffing and growling outside the shed door.

Sometimes Archie could hear the rotters fighting but he could never get to them.

So always listen carefully.

If you can ever hear tiny voices bickering all day long, your elves may just be meanies too....

ABOUT THE AUTHORS

Emily is seven. She likes dogs, maths and winning at board games.

Retired journalist Martin has advanced cystic fibrosis (CF) and wrote the bestselling Charlie Fry series to raise awareness about the life-limiting condition.
He writes children's books in his spare time, mainly, to keep away from the fridge and the Xbox.

His other work includes:

The Football Boy Wonder

The Demon Football Manager

The Magic Football Book

The Football Spy

The Football Superstar

The Football Boy Wonder Chronicles

The entire Charlie Fry Series is available via Amazon in paperback and Kindle today.

Martin has also written a Halloween story for older children:

The Pumpkin Code

Follow Martin on:

Facebook
Facebook.com/footballboywonder

Instagram
@charliefrybooks

ABOUT THE ILLUSTRATOR

Philip Knibbs is an illustrator with a background in comic book artwork.

Based in Bedfordshire, he lives with his wife, two daughters, a dog, a cat, three chickens and foster hedgehogs.

You can keep up with what he's currently working on at www.philbertz.com

COPYRIGHT

Printed in Great
Britain
by Amazon